Words to Know Before You Read

kangaroos
ketchup
key
kick
kids
kilometers
kiss
koalas
kookaburras

www.rourkeeducationalmedia.com

Edited by Precious McKenzie
Illustrated by Ed Myer
Art Direction, Cover and Page Layout by Tara Raymo

Library of Congress PCN Data

Kangaroo Country / J. Jean Robertson
ISBN 978-1-62169-240-9 (hard cover) (alk. paper)
ISBN 978-1-62169-198-3 (soft cover)
Library of Congress Control Number: 2012952735

Rourke Educational Media
Printed in the United States of America,
North Mankato, Minnesota

rourkeeducationalmedia.com

customerservice@rourkeeducationalmedia.com   •   PO Box 643328 Vero Beach, Florida 32964

Kangaroo Country

Counselor
Fred

Dock
Official

Grace

Sid

Effie

Bret

Andee

Cole

Yari

Written By J. Jean Robertson
Illustrated By Ed Myer

Counselor Fred yells, "Hey kids, did you hear? We get to go to Australia!"

"Where's that?" asks Grace.

"Down under," answers Sid.

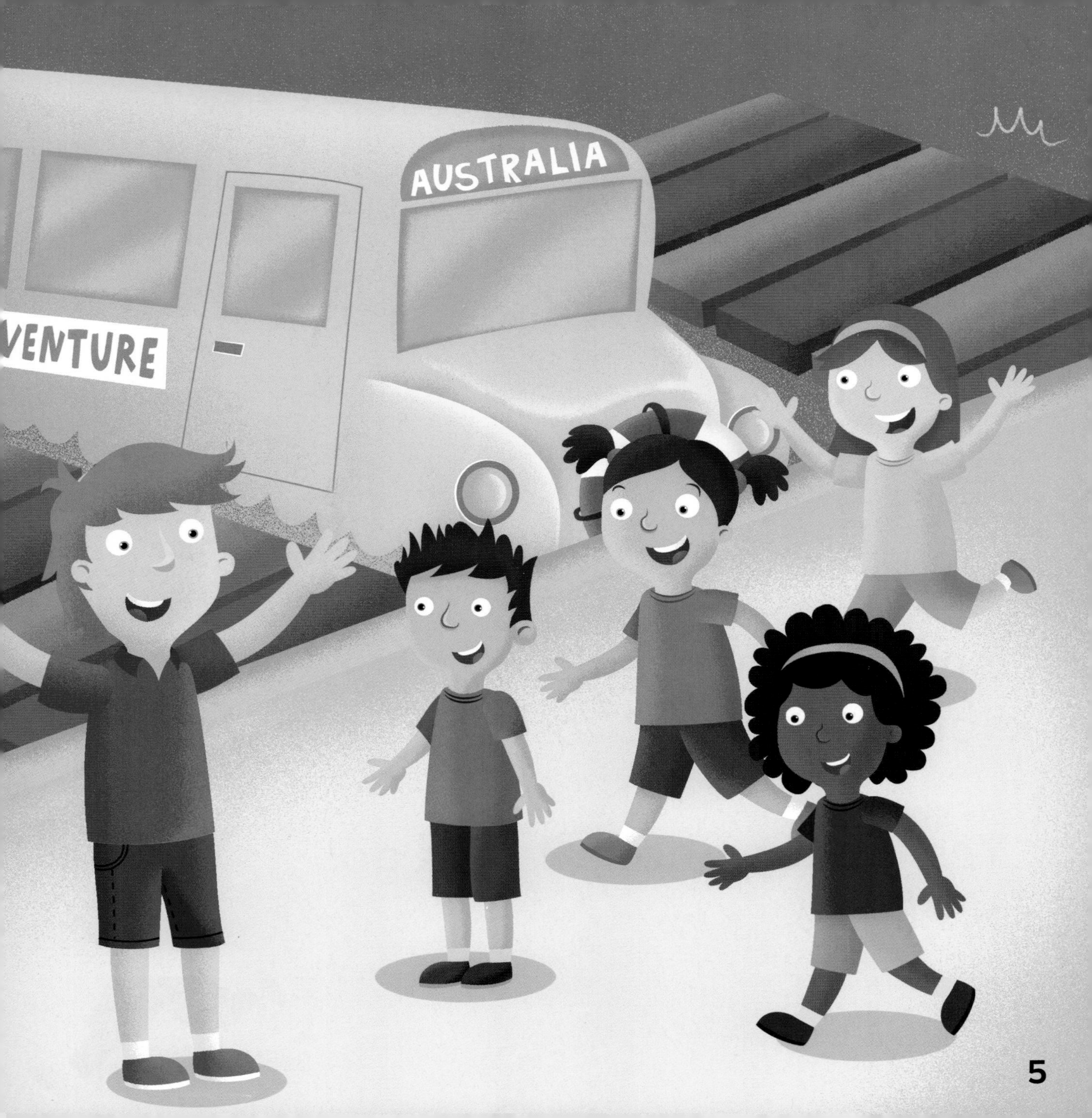
AUSTRALIA
VENTURE

"Isn't that many, many kilometers away?" asks Grace.

"Yes, so hop aboard! Let's go!" says Effie.

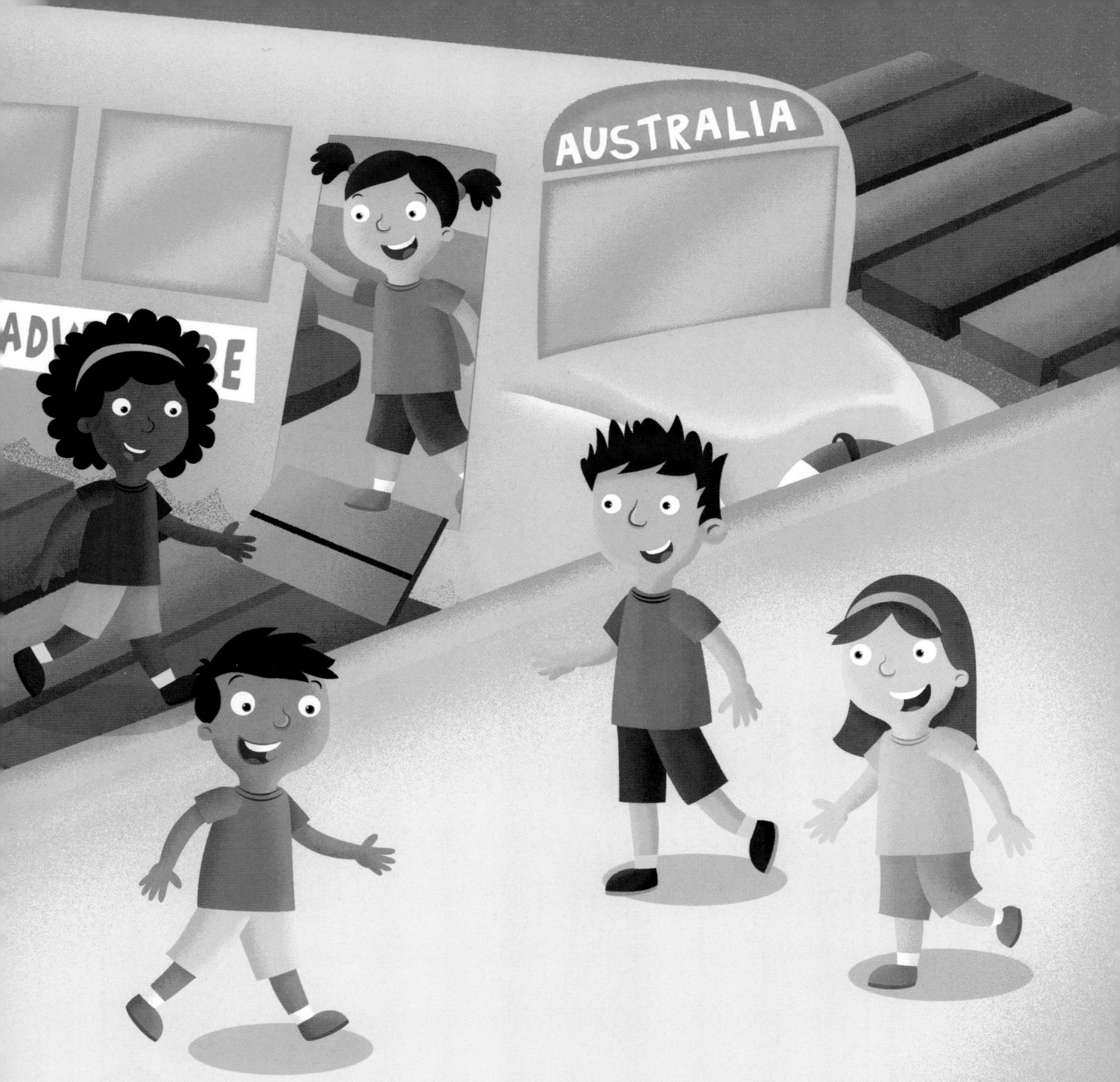
AUSTRALIA

"Good day, mates. Welcome to Australia, the land of kookaburras, koalas, and kangaroos," says the dock official.

Counselor Fred calls, "Kids, it's time to go off roading in the Outback. Take your key."

"What's the Outback?" asks Bret.

"We'll soon see," answers Counselor Fred.

"I see red dirt," says Effie.

"Looks like ketchup," sighs Bret.

"Are you hungry already?" asks Andee.

"Kangaroos," calls Sid.

"Some have joeys in their pockets," says Grace.

15

"I hear loud laughing," says Bret.

"Look, a kookaburra laughing at the boxing kangaroos!" shouts Effie.

"Watch out! That kangaroo might kick you," laughs Yari.

"Maybe those are koalas in the trees," says Sid.

"Do koalas kiss?" asks Andee.

"I think they are cleaning each other," answers Counselor Fred.

19

"I am glad we came to Australia," says Yari.

"I love kangaroo country!" says Bret.

After Reading Word Study

Picture Glossary

Directions: Look at each picture and read the definition. Write a list of all of the words you know that start with the same sound as *kiss*. Remember to look in the book for more words.

kangaroos (kang-guh-ROOZ): Kangaroos are marsupials with long, strong back legs and short front legs.

ketchup (KECH-uhp): Ketchup is a red sauce made from tomatoes. People like to use it on hamburgers and French fries.

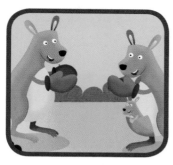

kick (KIK): When you kick something you hit it with your foot.

kids (KIDZ): Kids is a slang word for children.

kiss (KISS): When you place your lips on someone that is called a kiss. It is one way to show love.

koalas (koh-ah-luhz): Koalas are furry animals that look like small bears. They live in trees.

About the Author

J. Jean Robertson, also known as Bushka to her grandchildren and many other kids, lives in San Antonio, Florida, with her husband. She is retired after many years of teaching. She enjoys spending time with her family, traveling, reading, and writing books for children.

Ask The Author!
www.rem4students.com

About the Illustrator

Ed Myer is a Manchester-born illustrator now living in London. After growing up in an artistic household, Ed studied ceramics at university but always continued drawing pictures. As well as illustration, Ed likes traveling, playing computer games, and walking little Ted (his Jack Russell).